CAMP OUT

Written by
Sarah Toast

Cover illustrated by
Eddie Young

Interior illustrated by
Joe Veno

Louis Weber, C.E.O.
Publications International, Ltd.
7373 North Cicero Avenue
Lincolnwood, Illinois 60646

Manufactured in U.S.A.

8 7 6 5 4 3 2 1

ISBN: 0-7853-1070-3

PUBLICATIONS INTERNATIONAL, LTD.
Little Rainbow is a trademark of Publications International, Ltd.

David and Liz have work to do. After a long hike, they have arrived at the edge of the woods with all their camping gear packed in backpacks.

Now they have to pitch camp. First they stretch a rope between two trees and tie it tight. Then they make a tent out of the blanket they brought along.

David and Liz are hungry after hiking and setting up camp. They settle down in the tent and open their backpacks. They take out sandwiches and apples to eat for lunch. They drink grape juice from canteens.

David takes his binoculars out of his pack. Liz tells her brave teddy bear to guard the campsite while they go off to look for adventure.

David and Liz walk quietly so they can listen for wild animals.

"What's that?" asks David. He hears something in the bushes behind him. Liz hears it, too.

"Let's just keep walking," says Liz. When they look back, they see a tiger sneaking out of the bushes.

Liz and David walk for a long time. Just when they begin to get tired, they find sturdy branches that are just the right size for walking sticks.

They walk past a big log lying across their path. Liz sees something moving on the other side of the log.

Liz and David walk up to the log very quietly. On the other side is a white rabbit nibbling delicious grass. The rabbit looks at the two explorers, then it scampers away.

"We've seen a tiger and a rabbit," says David. "Let's look closely at the ground and find more wild animals."

David and Liz walk and look, but they don't see any more animals. Finally they find two beautiful blue feathers on the ground. Liz looks up to see where the feathers fell from.

"I see a bird's nest!" she exclaims. "The mother bird is taking care of three little baby birds."

"Let's get a closer look," says David. He gets the binoculars out of his pack so they can both see the birds better.

The explorers keep hiking until they come to a great lake—well, a pond, at least. Liz and David agree that crossing the pond will be tough.

First they take off their backpacks and slide the straps onto their walking sticks. Then they take off their shoes and socks and roll up their pants. They balance all their gear on their heads and fearlessly slosh from one shore of the lake—well, pond—to the other. The water feels cool to their feet and the mud feels good between their toes.

On the far side of the water, David and Liz sit down to let their feet dry before they put their shoes and socks back on. No sooner do they start exploring again, than they see something exciting.

"Muddy tracks!" says Liz.

"They look like bear tracks to me," says David.

The two trackers look at each other and think a minute before they decide. "Let's follow those tracks!" they both say.

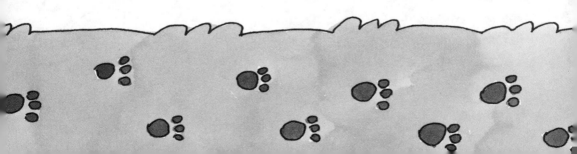

David and Liz follow the tracks through the grass. It gets harder and harder not to lose the trail. They stop in their own tracks when they see that the bear tracks lead right to their tent!

David laughs and runs to the tent. "Come on, Liz! This bear won't hurt us!" he says.

Just then they hear David's mom calling to them.

"Hi, little campers," says David's mom. "I thought I'd let Bingo out to play with you in the yard. He's waiting for you in the tent."

Bingo is David's new puppy.

Liz, David, and Bingo play in the tent for the rest of the day. "Let's build a rocket and fly to the moon tomorrow," says Liz. "I'll bring my binoculars," says David.